*Nurah's Diary*

# Love In Cancun

As-salam Alaelcum fatou,

May Allah light up your path. So sad I missed you on this trip.
love,

Ganiyah Tope Fajingbesi

ISBN: 978-0-9890868-2-0

*Your mind is the most powerful tool you own,*

*It is the inventor of your biggest miracles,*

*And the mother of your worst nightmare,*

*So, be protective of your thoughts,*

*Guard your dreams and possibilities,*

*And most of all, be mindful of who you allow to live rent-free in it.*

# *My Story*

My name is Nurah. I am 38 years old and single. Well, I think the right word to use may be divorced since I was married once, but I don't know if I should really count that marriage since it crashed like a pack of cards in two years and eight months. Anyway, I am sure you get the story about my status, so let's move on to my career.

I used to be a successful, highflying, busy executive racking up frequent flyer miles all over the United States doing some seriously important work that saved lives. No, I wasn't a doctor, but that is how my bosses and the public saw the work, I guess. The truth is that I was actually a stressed out, badly burnt out, and terribly bored accountant, too scared to walk away from a comfortable, six figure job with perks. I knew the job and travel was killing my spirit, especially after I lost my numero uno supporter and cheerleader, my father, late last year, but I just didn't know how to pack my bags and run like I did from my marriage four years ago. Each time I tried, my legs failed to move as quickly as my heart, so I stayed for six years, suffering and smiling.

But life was not all doom and gloom, there was

light in my heart sometimes, especially when I was not traveling or holed up in my Washington D.C office. My family, a few close friends, and opportunities to volunteer for charities I care about often brought me so much light and joy, but honestly, those were not enough to light up my entire world. So I prayed for strength like I had never done before, and, during the last month of Ramadan, the doors ultimately opened: my heart and my legs were in sync, and I reclaimed my life when I quit my job on August 21, 2015.

My decision to quit shocked a lot of people, who thought they knew me, but it was hardly a surprise to people in my inner circle—my best friend Zoe and my sisters Arin and Bola were not surprised at all. They had known this was coming, in fact they were glad when I finally "woman-ed" up to quit. What surprised them, however, is what I did immediately after my resignation. What is the first thing a newly unemployed person who doesn't have a lot of money does? If you guessed that I looked for, or started another job so that I could keep up with this "bills infested" American life, you are wrong. But if you guessed that I got on an airplane and headed for a vacation in Cancun then, yes, you guessed right.

I knew I needed some ocean breeze and space from technology, some time away from my apartment and even the people in my life who I love dearly. In short, I needed some *me* time. So off I went with no phones, no laptops or tablets, and wait for this—no camera. Yes, the picture loving Nurah went on vacation without a camera. Apart from a few clothes and a soul eager to reconnect with the Lord, the only other things I packed on the trip were a notebook and a pen. Six days of bliss sleeping in my room right on the ocean was just what the doctor recommended. The holiday would be great if I had a chance to relax, reconnect with my soul, spirit and my creator; but why settle for great when there is excellent? So I shot for an excellent vacation and that's exactly what I got. An excellent vacation is the one that sends you back home with the best memories, love and so much more. And that is what Cancun gave to me!

Good thing I took that pen and notebook because I kept a diary for you. So feel free to thank me when you experience this in Cancun, Banjul, Grenada, Seychelles or wherever else you decide to go to reconnect with your soul after reading my diary. I have included a page at the end of the book for you to begin writing your story too. So go ahead and speak life powerfully into your biggest dreams, then sit back and watch them come true. Be sure to let me know what worked for you at www.ganiyah.com.

PS: No better place to write than the ocean or seaside!

# *WHY?*

A diary is usually a private thing, but I am sharing mine with the world because the only things you truly own are the things you give away, and I want to own the hope and dreams I got in Cancun in August 2015.

❖ To show you that it is never too late to start again, to fall in love, to get your second chance or that big break.

❖ To testify that there can be miracles if you can bring yourself to believe.

❖ To tell you that real love will come into your life once you decide to love yourself unconditionally and embrace your fabulousness in spite of your flaws.

❖ To shatter myths and burst stereotypes related to faith, race, and ethnicity.

❖ To convince you that a solo vacation is long overdue and good for your soul.

❖ And hey! I am sharing this so you can have something nice and inspiring to read when you take that solo vacation that will wake your spirits up and connect you with your heart and soul.

I pray that I succeed in my mission to get you to unplug, sleep, pray, and connect in the most beautiful place you can find, even if that place is within the four walls of your home.

To my dad whose passing on November 11, 2014 shook me to my core; who I miss every day, but whose lesson to serve others and enjoy life I carry with me always.

Also dedicated to SD, my mom and my siblings.

And to the children we serve at United for Kids Foundation, the displaced people in Nigeria, Syria and all around the world, who, unlike me, cannot get on an airplane to escape their lives.

A very special thank you to Adaobi Oniwinde and Ganiyat Salami who graciously reviewed the manuscript. And to the talented and creative Timi Majekodunmi (SkratcHaus Studios) for creating the beautiful book cover.

*I honestly believe that every human being has two duties:*

*To find what they were created to do,*

*And then find the person who was created to help them do it.*

**-Tope Ganiyah Fajingbesi**

# Life

Don't measure your life by counting the days,

Measure it by the weight of your moments,

Not just the moments that take your breath away,

Or the ones that make your heart skip,

Measure your life by the moments you are present,

Each moment your heart shows up for is worth a lifetime.

Take a pause now and again,

To feel the magic in the swaying of the ocean,

The submission of the trees,

The victory of the sun despite dark clouds,

Then its own setting as decreed by its Lord.

And the gentle assurance in the moon's appearance,

To feel the romance between the stars and the night's breeze.

When you find the magical moments,

Be present to capture them,

Not with gadgets crafted by men,

But simply with the perfect harmony within you,

The one between your eyes and the depths of your heart,

Then you will have captured them forever.

# *Vamonos (Let's Go!)*

**Monday August 24th 2015**
**08:50 A.M.**
**Baltimore, Maryland USA**

It's Monday and I am relaxed and writing this note with a big smile on my face. You have to know that would have been a taboo a couple of days ago. Monday mornings meant I was either rushing to catch a flight or running to Odenton rail station to make sure I was on the 8:34 a.m. train before it left me. So, honestly, you couldn't catch me smiling on a Monday morning. But this Monday is different; the tides have turned. I am sitting in the airport shuttle, but, no, it's not what you think, this isn't a work related trip to the airport. I am with six other passengers, who aren't smiling, or shall I say grinning, like me; they must still be stuck in that life I left behind last week Friday. But, unlike them, I am not jetting off to some work meeting this week, I am on my way to Cancun to rest, relax, and kick off a new, and might I dream, my most beautiful chapter yet.

The Sky Priority lane at BWI was empty as expected when I arrived there, but, as usual, the man behind the counter asked me (with that look on his face as if he was expecting me to say, "I don't belong to the fast lane"), "Sky Priority or First Class?"

I replied, "Both actually." Yes, I may not have paid any actual dollars for this trip, but all these years of flying for work have certainly paid for these perks. And I am going to rock it to the maximum! The airport security line was also a breeze; the combination of Sky Priority and TSA pre-check, in spite of my hijab, allowed me access to walk through with as little fuss as possible and with my shoes on. There are actually a few benefits of being a frequent flyer I tell you.

## 12:50 P.M.

Now in Atlanta, about to make my connection to Cancun, and I see so many folks on their phones and laptops, some on work teleconferences in fact. Wow! They all seem so tense; I feel sorry for them. Is this how you all used to look at me when I was still stuck in that rut? Thank you, God, for rescuing me from that sad life.

Anyway, here I go! Six days of love, life, laughter,

and relaxation. No phones, no social media, no email; just me, the ocean, my life, and love. This bliss right here, right now, can only be a gift from God. Two hours and we will be on the ground, insha Allah.

And guess what? Now that I am on the plane, I am not as nervous about the fact that I am not taking a camera as I was while finding my way to Cancun boarding gate E9. I have done trips without my laptop, phone, and email, but this is the first time I am going without a camera. I honestly dilly-dallied on the no camera decision for a long time. How do I capture the memories? What will I have to flip through when I want to re-live this vacation? But that's the whole point of this no camera angle. I want the moments to be captured by my heart, that way I will have them forever. What I have found is that we lose the magic while trying to capture each moment with technology. Our brains shut down when our eyes and our hearts aren't in sync and present. So I am going to try to be there, to live and breathe Cancun, more than I did Charleston in 2012, Puerto Rico in 2013, or San Diego in 2014. I will certainly look for beach and street photographers to take one or two memorable photos for me, but I am not going to lose the magic trying to capture every moment, I will entrust that job to my heart this time.

## 03:30 P.M.
## In Cancun

I knew I had made the right choice picking

Cancun as soon as I stepped out of the airport to the warm embrace of the freshly created cool breeze, which rushed out to greet me with open arms in spite of the hot weather. My heart instantly recognized the understated beauty and peacefulness of this tourist haven. The warm and beautiful feeling you get when you step out of Cancun's modest airport is completely different from what happens when you step out of my two home airports: Murtala Muhammed airport in Lagos, which injects several shots of stress into the veins of the unsuspecting and unprepared sojourner, and the more modern and sprawling yet stress-inducing Washington-Dulles International airport. The courtyard of the airport was small, and the smooth road leading out to the world of calmness had only two modest lanes, but it was gorgeously lined with beautiful palm trees that didn't tire from caressing the faces of arriving passengers. The streets were clean and smooth, and the people, even those selling all sorts of packages—time-shares, tours, and everything under the sun—managed to ooze calmness and relaxation while carrying on with their trade. My heart joined my eyes in a big smile as I read the beautiful signs welcoming visitors and promising paradise as we drove out of the airport. This was going to be an amazing week for sure! The ride from the airport to the resort took less than 30 minutes; the driver from USA Transfers was warm and welcoming. He obviously knew the town well and spent the better part of the journey telling me in broken English all the cool places I must not miss over the next six days.

He pointed out the imposing and very beautiful,

all white RIU Palace Las Americas as soon as we were close to the hotel. Wow! The photos I saw online were beautiful, but honestly, they didn't do this breathtaking hotel the justice it really deserves. I was still trying to take in the outer beauty of this amazing palace when it unleashed its real beauty—its people. From the friendly bellman who opened the car door to let me out of the taxi and then proceeded to take my small luggage, to the lady who greeted me with the sweetest tasting non-alcoholic drink on the planet as soon as I stepped into the lobby, the message was clear: I was going to be royalty for the next six days. And honestly, I didn't have a problem with that!

Ganiyah Tope Fajingbesi

# Dear Diary

*To capture a powerful moment forever*
*Set your eyes on a blind date with your heart.*
*To give life to your most beautiful dreams*
*Create a lasting love affair between your pen and paper.*

My suite on the fourth floor was more beautiful than I imagined it would be, but, honestly, it was not the things in the room —the comfortable bed and luxurious bathroom—that caught my heart, it was what was outside that blew my mind. I stepped onto the balcony and there it was —the best view ever. The Atlantic Ocean in its glory and splendor was right there and all mine for the next six days. I closed my eyes to allow my mind to connect to the power of the incredible space my feet stood on.

If the dreams in Cancun must come alive after

this vacation, I had to keep a diary. I unpacked my pen and paper from my luggage.

And so the diary begins…

## At Sunset

I left my watch in the room so I am not sure what time it is right now, but the beautiful view of the sunset, soothing sound of the waves, and the gentle ocean breeze caressing my face are giving me the most amazing feeling I have had in a long time.

Lovers were strolling in and out, but the beach is now quiet because I am the only one sitting here. Imagine, I have a whole beach in Cancun to myself, even if it's just for a few minutes. This is all so beautiful. I would have been taking pictures left, right, and center to preserve these moments, to make sure they never go away, but I don't have a camera, remember? I have got something more powerful than a camera. My brain has this all sorted out and saved for eternity. No camera can feel the touch of the ocean breeze and no amount of megapixels can capture what the eyes behold at sunset on a beautiful beach in Cancun. Using technology to hold it still and make it last is really nothing but injustice to the soul, an unfair disruption of a divine encounter between the heart and the brain.

It's getting dark now, I am going to my suite to say my prayers, and then perhaps I will come down for the entertainment show at the theater. Tomorrow should be an easy day, nothing but lounging until the dinner cruise. I may go to Chichén Itza on Wednesday, I really don't want to go because it's quite far but everyone says it's a must-see in Mexico. Also, the tour agent I saw today, Juan Jose, did an awesome job convincing me. Hey! I might as well enjoy everything Mexico has to offer me this week. Then I will do a photo shoot on Thursday, insha Allah (if God wills), only I have no idea what I am going to wear for the occasion, but I am sure there is something in my tiny suitcase that will work.

## 10:30 p.m.

Day 1 in Cancun is almost over. So glad I am doing this for me. I feel so liberated already.

Ganiyah Tope Fajingbesi

## Ask Him

Remember your Lord always,

Ask of Him shamelessly,

Without reservations,

Or restrictions,

Ask from Him alone,

Have high expectations,

For He is the best compensator,

And the best compensation,

All in One.

# Can This Moment Last Forever?

**Tuesday August 25th 2015**
**06:49 A.M.**

I just had the most amazing and soul lifting dhikr (worship) session on my hotel room balcony. I was about to step out of the room to continue connecting with my Creator on the beach when my room phone rang. And, yes, you guessed right! It was my sister Bola calling, and the first thing she said was, "Oh! So you think you can escape from us, right?" That got both of us cracking up. She told me that, as expected, she and Arin have been trying to reach me despite the fact that I told them this was a vacation to unplug from both loved and unloved ones. But did I really think she was going to let me fully unplug for six whole days? This is the sister who usually wonders why she hasn't heard from me in a long while if I don't call her on my way to the office on any weekday. But I was really happy to hear her voice; I spoke with her before leaving Baltimore yesterday, but it seemed like we hadn't talked for many days! She filled me in on her vacation and got me up to date on the latest stories from the home front. The giggles and laughter certainly gave my morning a powerful boost, but I sent her packing to continue my journey right after telling her she has to come here with Ruffy, her husband.

Okay now, off to my "Walk with God" and, again, I am so thankful I don't have my camera or phone. I am now realizing that in the process of trying to capture a moment on film, we miss out on the opportunity to capture it in our hearts, which is a more permanent storage than any device. I am stepping out in my black robe with glitters and hijab. Of course, everyone will stare at me; who goes on the beach wearing this much clothing, all covered up? But perhaps it will be a teachable moment for anyone who cares to learn that you don't have to be naked to feel the breeze and embrace of the ocean on your soul, and that women in hijab aren't mysterious creatures.

If you want to connect with love, your soul, and spirit, nothing beats the ocean, not even mountains come close.

Not sure what time it is, as there is only one visible clock in this resort, and it is in the lobby. In fact, if you don't look carefully, you will miss it. I just had breakfast, and it was such a blissful experience.

Of course, I received a few stares from folks as I dug my heels into the soft, white sand on the beach. I can't blame them at all, when was the last time they saw a woman in full Muslim garb, especially a black one, on the beach? The ones staring probably associate blackness with poverty and suffering thanks to CNN, and the hijab with oppression and terrorism, thanks to Fox News. So seeing me walking the beach and living the same life they are living is probably as strange as it gets, but trust me to meet their stares with "Holas" and big smiles.

I ate breakfast sitting across the table from a lady who was on her smartphone most of the time. I felt quite sorry for her; to be trapped in jail when you are on vacation has to be a tragedy, and the worst part was she probably had no idea she was in chains. I felt like going over to tap her into reality, I wanted to put my hands around her and tell her, "Sweetie, put the shackles away and embrace freedom," but, of course, I couldn't do that. Why? Well, this is my vacation too; I'm not here to save anyone but myself.

After breakfast, I walked over to the tour operator's area and, of course, my friend Juan Jose, the one who sold me on the Chichen Itza tour yesterday, was there to greet me with a smile. But instead of selling the Chichen Itza tour to me, he told me to buy it from the gray line operator who had not been available when I came down to look for him yesterday. He said in the sweetest voice ever, "We are buddies who work on commission; I would like him to make something today since he was not here yesterday." Wow! There are still kind people in the world, not just the cutthroat and greedy folks who seem to litter the streets these days.

His buddy was nice too; I asked him where he was from and he said Acapulco. You know what my excited response was? "Acapulco? Do you know Maria de Los Angeles?" He laughed heartily and we began talking about growing up in Nigeria watching Mexican TeleNovelas, which I don't get to watch in the U.S. because they are not subtitled there. He asked me for my room number and, in my new Spanish wannabe accent, I replied, "Quatro uno dos."

He replied in English, "Four one twelve?"

I said, "Si."

Bye-bye, Nurah from Baltimore; Hola Nurah De Cancun, Vamonos!

As I walked back to my room to take a morning nap and to continue dancing in my dreams to the cool soundtrack of the ocean breeze, I knew that this trip was exactly what my soul needed. It didn't matter what the future held, what was important was the realization that life is not measured by the days we spend, but the moments our hearts truly experience. Amen! And this moment right here will stay in my heart forever.

## 01:20 P.M.

I just got out of bed, even though I have been

awake for about 40 minutes. What's the hurry? This feels so good, so different from regular life, just what my soul needs. No urgency to do anything, no phones ringing, no emails to send my day south, and, even though I felt a tinge of guilt about it this morning when I was so confused and spoilt for choice at the breakfast buffet, I am honestly glad there are no reminders of the poor people I owe a duty of care to here.

Hmmm, did I just write that I owe poor people a duty of care? Why did I use those words? Is the charitable work I do an obligation? Is that how I see the children's foundation I run with Iria and Manni? Okay, okay, okay! Maybe sometimes I see it that way. I have to tell you, it can be quite overwhelming seeing so much need, and then feeling the handicap of not being able to solve the problems, and, to make matters worse, everyone refers cases they see on the street, social media, or in their neighborhood to us. I think the better way to say it is that everyone dumps sad cases and bags of guilt on our chests via email, social media, phone calls and even physically. I tell you that this can drain all the joy from your day before it even starts.

So to be free from all that, even for just six days, is blissful. I know the energy I get from here will equip me with the arsenal to fight when I return to real life. But for now, standing on the balcony staring at the ocean, in its heavenly beauty and its stripes of blue and green, is the only agenda my head has to handle.

Indeed, this is it. This is what it means to fall in love, real love. I am falling in love and enjoying every bit of the process.

## At Los Arco Restaurant
## 02:40 P.M.

I will never understand why westerners eat three meals at the same time. Yes people; appetizers, entree, and dessert are three meals in one sitting. I just had so much of the yummy Italian bread and I am so full already. You are probably wondering what business I have eating white bread. Yeah, no dieting in Cancun, my dear! But hey! I am going to eat the yummy looking salad. Oh, yes! I now eat raw leaves, *me*—that same Nigerian girl who could not eat cold raw leaves when I first moved to America. (Sigh.) That's what happens when you want to maintain your figure in the land of plenty food. Sorry, I digressed—anyway, the main course and dessert are still coming. You should see the dessert spread, all laid out right there close to the door so you can't escape no matter how stuffed you are. Not to worry, I will be having some cake and ice cream for sure.

Still staring at the yummy looking desert spread, my mind recalls the look on the face of the greeter when I walked in; it wasn't quite pity or shock, but it was something in the middle of the two I saw on his face when I responded that I was the only one dining. People think a solo vacation is like punishment for a crime. If only they knew it is actually a reward for the soul.

You know, those know-it-all Americans can really learn a thing or two from Mexicans! The TV in the suite is not in the bedroom, but in the living area so the bedroom is reserved for sleeping and relaxing, and there are no dogs running around the entire place scaring and stealing from the experience of non-dog lovers like me. Speaking of TV, I thought to switch on the one in my suite to see what sort of things they watch here, and it was Fox News that greeted me with the story of some Americans who saved lives on a train going to France from Belgium. Some "Muslim" man had a gun and was trying to do whatever it was he had planned when the brave guys took him down. If only the so-called Muslims that go around killing people realize that they do nothing but make life difficult for millions of innocent Muslims, perhaps they would stop. Maybe not. And the guy is from Africa. Since when did we begin these sorts of "misadventures"? An African Muslim trying to kill people in Europe? I just shake my head. Life and its mysteries. Well, so much for trying to see what's on Mexican TV. What did I think I would find? Reruns of *Maria de Los Angeles* or *The Rich Also Cry*? Okay, no more TV, which was more than enough.

## On The Beach
## 04:30 P.M.

I just realized another thing that Americans can

learn from Mexicans: stop putting clocks everywhere! Being constantly reminded of the time adds insane pressure to our already stressed-out lives! There is just an amazing and refreshing feeling you get watching time pass naturally, only getting help from the sun and the moon. It is such a beautiful feeling.

Oh, by the way, being fully dressed on the beach when everyone is practically naked doesn't feel as weird as I feared it would. But, honestly, the verse in the Quran that says to lower one's gaze must have been revealed for situations like this. Arghhhh! Everyone is practically naked; thank God I don't feel the need to stare or even look at whatever it is they feel the need to display.

## 05:00 P.M.

Still on the beach, and this is one of those rare times when I miss having a camera. My quiet moment in spite of the swimmers making splashes in front of me was interrupted by the sound of a middle-aged man hawking stuff on the beach. It wasn't his announcement of "cold cold mangoes" as he walked by that interrupted the "noisy silence" I was experiencing prior to his arrival, but the fact that he had his wares—a couple of bottles—in a bucket on his head. It just reminded me of home; home as in Nigeria, not Baltimore. A place where, in spite of its chaos, my heart will always reside, and recognize as its roots.

I am sitting on the beach with Jesus from the

resort spa who is trying to sell me on some package. He is selling the spa services with so much passion, obviously trying to make his daily quota, but I can't get past his name. Why don't African parents name their children Jesus? Does he feel pleased or special when he is in church and the congregation start calling Jesus Christ? I eventually reserved a package for Friday, partly because I felt guilty for having a separate monologue in my mind while he was pitching the sale and partly because a spa treatment was part of the Cancun vacation plans anyway. In any case, how could I not buy something from a guy named Jesus?

Just took my eyes off my notepad for a split second and, behold, there is a fine black man making his way here. Oh! Nurah, lower your gaze! Okay, okay, okay, back to my notes.

The education you get sitting on a beach on a Mexican evening cannot even be paid for. There is a young girl sitting next to me trying to take selfies but she can't seem to get a look that makes her happy. She keeps trying on different hats and checking herself out endlessly, but she can't seem to settle on a look that's gorgeous enough for her standards. Poor soul, it must be tough to live like that. All of this work just to take a selfie? Pray tell me what in the world she would do if this was a real photo shoot for a magazine the entire world would see?

The sight of hawkers on the beach is no longer thrilling. I can now see that's a common thing here, but no one has put their wares on their heads like the first hawker. The selfie girl has now stood up and another friend in a bikini is taking pictures of her. Honestly, if this is not a shoot for a modeling job, I don't understand why it has been this much hard work (laughs). I am officially bored with all their vanity already. Thank God for a better distraction, two kids playing in the sand, looking so happy and joyful. That's what life should be about—simple and stress free.

The ocean is getting nosier; that's my cue to stop writing and get back to reading *The First Warm Evening of the Year* by Jamie M. Saul.

## 06:00 P.M.

I am back in room 412, and I have bad news for Jesus, the sales guy from the hotel spa—I am cancelling my Friday appointment, I got a better deal. I just saved $90 by crossing the road, yes literally. I was going in search of an ATM that dispensed United States Dollars (USD) so that I could pay for the spa package Jesus sold to me on the beach when I saw the signpost for another spa, which had a "Trip Advisor Winner of Excellence" sign. Not only did a massage and facial cost just $100 instead of the hotel's $190, they also take American Express, which is beginning to sound like a miracle up here. Anyway, I have a date with them on Thursday. Sorry Mr. Jesus, I am going with Bamboo Spa. I still love you though.

I rode up the elevator with a lovely couple and as soon I saw how warm, friendly, and happy they were

I knew that they were Americans. Say what you want about Americans, but no other people come remotely close when it comes to warmth and friendliness. We chatted a bit about Arizona, their home state and it made me miss home; this time home is Baltimore, Maryland in the USA, not Lagos, Nigeria. Nigeria will always be where my heart lies, but the U.S.? Let's just say that has my head firmly in its grip. You can't live most of your adult life in a place and not fall in love with it, can you? I am certainly lucky to belong to two of the best, yet "misunderstood" countries in the world.

Now it's time to get ready for the sunset cruise, woo hoo! Watch out Cancun! Nurah is taking over… Vamonos!

## 06:45 P.M.

Leaving for the sunset cruise now and I am all decked out in my back halter neck dress. Okay, let me stop you before your mind lands you in the wrong place. The dress is halter neck quite alright, but I am wearing a black layering tee to cover up. And, of course, I brightened it all up with a beautiful pink hijab, a gold watch, bracelet, and gold sandals. I looked in the mirror and gave myself a nod of approval. Let's go, Cancun! No, no, this is Mexico, so it's Vamonos Cancun!

I stepped outside the lobby to wait for the shuttle where there were three other couples already waiting. I didn't want to badge into their party, so I stood aside like the solo traveler that I was. But one of the guys wasn't having any of that. Not only did I know he was American because of his bubbly personality, the warm and friendly drawl I picked up from his accent when he spoke gave him away as someone from one of the southern states. He asked if I was by myself, and when I said yes, he invited me to join their little fold. They all introduced themselves and we chatted heartily until the neat, mid-sized shuttle bus picked us up. Another couple joined us, and one guy who my eye had caught sometime during the day hopped on the bus too, and guess what? He came alone, thank goodness! No, it's not what you are thinking. I am not in Cancun to pick up a man. I am just happy I am not the only solo traveler in town.

As we stepped onto the beautiful boat, I paid close attention to the beautiful music blaring from the speaker, and it truly spoke to me. "*I try to carry the weight of the world, but I only have two hands.*" The singer must have had me in mind when he composed that one because the song had my name written all over it! That was honestly my cue to relax and enjoy the cruise and indeed the entire vacation. After all, I am in Cancun for six days and the world hasn't stopped moving because of it.

The cruise was quite short, but awesome! It was nice to see the entire city at night with all the beautiful lights and a warm breeze. I was already relaxed before the cruise, but now I am even more relaxed. Honestly, I have to find a way to do this every six months. To get away from life's chaos, especially for someone like me whose schedule is hectic from the first minute of the day till midnight, is not a luxury, it is a necessity.

Remember the Americans that I met in the elevator, Jeff and Laura from Arizona? We ended up sitting together during the cruise, and we had so much fun! I absolutely enjoyed their company. They have been married for 35 years, yet you would think they were newlyweds. Not just because they both looked young, but the way they touched each other even unconsciously, and were so friendly and playful with each other, you would think they just got married or even just recently met. It was totally amazing to watch and feel such love. Laura is a hairdresser and Jeff is a construction contractor, and they have grandkids. Now check this out, 35 years and still going strong, you would think they dated for a long time, knew for certain they were soul mates before taking the plunge. But no way, I asked how long they knew each other before marriage and Laura's response almost made me fall off my seat: "I knew him for three months before I became pregnant with our son. I had our son on December 18th and we got married the following December 13th. People were taking bets at our wedding thinking we weren't going to last." Sitting with Laura and Jeff will help you understand that the concept of soul mates is real. I honestly believe that finding your purpose goes beyond finding the career that makes you happy and fulfilled, it also includes, and very importantly too, finding and connecting with your soul mate, that ride-or-die person who will be there by your side whether the waves are gentle or not. But before you go in search of your ride-or-die man, you have got to know, love and embrace yourself first, otherwise you will miss the most beautiful gift because of its dull wrapper or go home with Mr. Nightmare wrapped in glossy sheets.

As we headed back to the hotel after the cruise, Jeff stopped to make yet another friend, and Laura and I just stood there laughing our heads off. This guy must be the friendliest soul on the planet. I told Laura I was going to write about both of them in my diary, which I was thinking of publishing, and Laura said, "When, not if, you become a famous writer, you will remember the crazy Americans you met in Cancun." And I corrected her, I told her that, fun, warm and inspiring, not crazy, would be my choice of words when describing both of them. They certainly added color to my holiday for sure.

---

Okay, time to pray, eat, and head to the theater for tonight's show.

# The Race

*The dead man is not the soulless case lying in a coffin,*

*The dead man is the breathing case who wastes his soul,*

*Running around the world with no dreams,*

*Having nothing to aspire to but his sojourn in the grave.*

# *His Son Stole My Heart*

## Wednesday August 26ᵗʰ 2015
## 09:30 A.M.

I was too tired to write by the time I returned to my room last night. I have to be honest, it wasn't really physical weakness; God knows I have not felt any of the back, head, neck, or other pains that often dampened my regular life when I was working and traveling with the American Federation of Teachers (AFT,) my previous employer. At first, I had trouble figuring out why my soul felt so tired; after all, I was on a relaxing vacation. In actual fact, I'd just had a fun time on the sunset boat cruise with Jeffrey and Laura and I enjoyed the couples' show at the resort theater. So why did I feel so drained of energy? The cause of my fatigue finally hit me as I walked out of the theater after the show. I was mentally tired because I was solo, not only on vacation, but in my real life too. It's one thing to get away once in a while from your spouse on a solo trip, but knowing that, even after this whole solo getaway, there was no one to really go back to got me a little tired up there. Why are some people able to figure out this "happy" married life business and I just can't? There was the couple on the cruise last night, Jeffrey and Laura, who are still playful after 35 years of marriage. There were the contestants at the entertainment show: the veterans (33 years) who emerged as the Riu Palace couple of the week, the biracial couple from Boston who have been married for eight years. They taught me that winning wasn't the most important part of competing, but having fun and being present in the moment was, because the more anxious I felt for them after they lost each of the three rounds the more at ease and happy they seemed. They were just having a nice time with each other. Then there were the young ones who had only been married for 15 months. In short, the stage had the entire spectrum of people who seemed to be able to hold this marriage business down. So what's wrong with me?

As I switched off the bedside lamp and pulled the sheets tight around me, I realized that one of the enemies that I was in Cancun to conquer and get away from had somehow found its way into my vacation luggage. I needed to throw it out of my heart quickly before it ruined my Cancun experience. Thank goodness, I signed up for the Chichen Itza tour, and it was on that note that I sent myself to the land of dreams.

This drive from Cancun to Chichen Itza reminds me so much of the commute from Lagos to my father's hometown in Southwestern Nigeria—Ijebu—but this road has fewer bumps. Well, that's not really true, this one has no bumps and zero traffic. Its natural beauty enhanced by mature trees is still intact unlike the Lagos-Ibadan expressway in Nigeria that has been assaulted by all sorts of buildings.

## 11:00 A.M.

Most of the bus was asleep when we arrived at Chichen Itza, one of the wonders of the world and a UNESCO designated archaeological site. The closer we got to our destination, the more anxious I became because I worried that the trip might be a complete waste of time. I love history, but I am not one to be wowed by stones and ancient looking attire. But you should have seen my eyes when I stepped off the bus! My heart literally stopped beating at the sight of the things my eyes beheld. Forget Chichen Itza, the first wonder of the world was right here in front of me. It wasn't until he said, "As Salam Alaekum," a sweet greeting of peace, that I was jolted back to reality. I felt like I had been standing still and staring at this divine wonder of the world for hours, but the reality was it was barely a minute. I must have been stuck on the same spot right outside the bus just staring at this amazing work of art because I suddenly realized that everyone on our tour had begun snapping photos of the sights, as in the real ones we came to see. Well, mine was right here at the entrance of the tour bus, as though he had been waiting for me to arrive.

Our tour guide began saying something in English, but, honestly, I could not hear a single word. The only thing I heard was the sweet greeting of peace and blessings from the masculine wonder of the world. I responded likewise and found that my throat had suddenly gone dry. "My name is Habeeb."

I should have responded but I was struggling to stop staring and, all of a sudden, my high functioning brain couldn't process more than one task at the same time. I was again jolted back to reality by my new friend. "Do you speak English? Hablo Espanol?"

"I am so sorry, yes, I speak English. This place is quite fascinating," I quickly stammered and hoped he believed that it was the Mayan wonderland that captivated me and not his presence.

"Where are you from?"

His reply gave me life. "USA. Maryland, USA."

"Wow! Really? I am from Nigeria but I live in the USA as well, Maryland too actually," I said.

"No kidding, it's nice to meet you." He ended with a long pause that made his words sound like a quiz. It was then that I realized I hadn't told him my name. "My name is Nurah," I said, almost apologizing. I needed to get myself together quickly. This wasn't looking good. I was not staring at him, but his presence was certainly affecting me.

"I assume you are staying in Cancun?" he asked with some hope in his eyes.

I said, "Yes."

"So how was your drive down here?"

"To be honest, it was like driving to some countryside in Nigeria. It was full of ancient people, stray, malnourished dogs, houses with thatched roofs and broken doors."

His hearty laughter was interrupted by the voice of our tour guide asking me to join the rest of the group.

Oops! I almost forgot the reason I came here.

"I better run along now, it was nice to meet you, Habeeb."

"The pleasure is all mine, Nurah. Enjoy the tour."

"Thank you very much."

My heart tumbled as I watched him walk away. I would have easily flipped the script on this tour in a heartbeat. Who needed history lessons and talks about ancient stones when the only wonder of the world was right here? Oh well...

---

We are a couple of minutes into the tour and the "wonder boy" is nowhere in sight. He must have gone off with his party some place in this massive, ancient land. What did I think would happen? He was going to leave his agenda and begin following a strange woman he ran into around the place? Get a grip, Nurah!

There are people talking, hawkers trying to sell tourists all sorts of things, but time must have frozen at that moment I met Habeeb. There was just something so enchanting about that man. But what if he was here with his wife and seven kids? Okay, maybe not seven kids, but two or three. Okay, maybe just him and his wife.

Focus, Nurah, focus!

There is a lot that we don't know about the world we live in and the people we share it with! Can you imagine that one and a half million people live around the Mayan land? As our tour progressed, especially as we began to see the "palapas", which are mud houses with thatched roofs, I wondered why Nigeria could not grab this obvious income-generating opportunity. We also have this history, these traditional worshippers, ancient culture and people, don't we? This is what Mexico is selling to us for $125 per person. If we begin ferrying people from Lagos so they can experience the rich cultural heritage available in abundance in Ijebu, Benin, or Ile-Ife, or even take Abeokuta more seriously, we may actually have a good shot at getting out of the sticky third world. In fact, forget the ancient tours. What if, instead of building Eko Atlantic, the Lagos government built a Cancun-like ocean-driven tourist town? Is that not what America, Jamaica, Bahamas, and now Mexico are selling? Wake up, Africa!

We had been walking around Chichen Itza for half an hour, and something about the ancient place, the paths, trees, and plantations reminded me of Ijebu, my father's hometown. A place he loved so much, which he wanted us to love as well, but somehow we didn't. The smell of the site was the same as daddy's favorite place, where his journey to his creator literally began when he suffered a stroke on October 4th 2014, the day that should have been a day of celebration – the festive day of Eid Adha. I was about to give in to my emotions, unpack yet another sorrow from my luggage, when that sweet voice interrupted my thoughts, more like rescued me from distress.

"I hope you are enjoying the tour."

*Wow! It was Habeeb again.* My heart leapt with unspeakable joy!

I was about to answer with relief in my heart when the cutest boy ran to him, holding his left leg as though he was shy. There was a stranger barging in on his bonding time with his dad, and he was there to give notice. This cute little boy was clearly his son; the resemblance was striking.

I knew it! How could this fine guy, who appeared to be in his 30s, be single and childless? Oh well! There goes my heart in the dumpster yet again.

I took my mind off him and his son for a couple

of seconds to hear Roberto, our tour guide, describe the special status of Mayan women who died during childbirth, warriors who died in war or people who died during human sacrifice (the Mayan tradition, just like Yoruba ancient tradition includes elements of human sacrifice).

"Come on, be nice, and say hello to Aunty."

You won't believe what happened next, which, from the look on Habeeb's face, shocked him more than it did me. I would not have missed a beat if not for the look on his face, in fact. I swear it was as though he had just heard the voice of a ghost when he said, "Hello Mama," while he wrapped his tiny, loving arms around my legs. I reached out to lift him up and something about that moment felt so natural, so beautiful. It felt just right as it took my mind back to five years ago when my darling unborn child constantly gave me hugs from the safety of my womb. I get hugs from children in my life all the time, but none ever took me back to Rahmah, my daughter that never was. That moment, which lasted for all of 30 seconds, must have felt like 30 minutes until Habeeb interrupted it with, "Okay buddy, let's run along now." His words felt rushed; I heard some anxiety in his voice too. It was as if he had heard or seen a ghost.

This time, there was no invitation in his voice again or the eagerness to know me, which I had heard when I first met him near my bus. What I heard now was an eagerness to get away. The only explanation I could come up with was that his wife must have made eye contact with him somewhere in the crowd, and they had to hurry back to her. It couldn't be that he was mad that his son called me mama, or could it? That was the most innocent and soulful connection ever. Why did he think he had a right to snatch that away from us?

"Us" Nurah? Are you serious? When did a stranger's son who mistakenly called you mama become us?

I had absolutely no opportunity to wallow in my second heartbreak of the day because my eyes beheld the most beautiful sight that distracted my heart—the kukulcan castle. Oh my goodness! Its size, the magnificence, and the way it beautifully rests against the blue skies like a backdrop in a carefully set photo wiped my invisible tears. This pyramid was one of the most amazing things any eye could behold on this hot and humid Mexican day. But just when I thought I had seen all there was to see about this wonder castle, I got a glimpse into the city underneath it. Yes, you read it right—a city, an entire city under this castle. Unbelievable!

No wonder my friend Bim said that I had to go on this particular tour that's turning out to be one of the most fascinating tours I have ever taken. As if the sight of the pyramid wasn't intriguing enough, the pyramid also has acoustic effects: You clap your hands and the pyramid responds with a cockcrow-like sound. Amazing!

Looking at the carvings and artifacts on display

here reminds me of the ancient Yoruba and Benin kingdoms. Roberto began talking about the Equinox, which I didn't quite understand, but all I could think about was my conviction that the Chinese didn't discover the world, and the white man didn't either; I think the world began in Africa.

But how can we even prove this when no one has access to the culture and powerful sights that can prove my point beyond words? Oh well…

---

Quite fascinating fact—The life expectancy of Mayan men back in the day was 45 and women 38; which Roberto said was better than Europe with a life expectancy of 24. Many Mayan men died of dental infections and the women primarily died from osteoporosis due to too many childbirth episodes. Aren't we lucky today?

## 02:00 P.M.

While walking to the restaurant for lunch, I heard some words that sounded like music to my ears. No, it wasn't Habeeb and his boy. It was a woman talking to another in front of a stall, and her words were, "*Elo lo so pe oun fe ta iyen?*" These words, spoken in my native dialect, Yoruba, mean, "How much did he say he wants to sell that for?" I always expect to find Nigerians everywhere I go, after all, we are 170 million people scattered all over the globe. But I was so sure no Nigerian would be here apart from me! Don't get me wrong, my people love to seek knowledge, but this place is quite a far distance from "our" usual vacation spots. Of course, I broke away from my party to chat with my fellow Nigerians before happily hopping along for lunch. That felt really good! Seeing "my people" outside our shores never gets old.

Lunch was absolutely delicious. It fit the theme of this entire place, which was fresh and enjoyable as well as natural. This is how human beings are supposed to live, it was exactly what Roberto and I were discussing while I was waiting for lunch to be served—how, in our bid to modernize the world, we have made our world less human and we are now paying dearly for it with sickness and conflicts. What a tragedy! My mind compared the scenes I had just experienced during the tour, the pace, the contentment in the beings we encountered, to the fast pace, conflict, and confusion in Washington, DC— just a three hour flight away, yet a world of difference between the two places. Really every one of us owes it to ourselves to pause, take a break, and refocus on what really matters once in every short while; to ask ourselves which is more important, to make a living or to make a life, then see how our everyday moments are working in alignment with our goal.

Speaking of taking breaks, I just took a break from writing in my diary to play with Lucas, my new four-year-old friend, a very happy kid from Los Angeles. Lucas, a beautiful blend of his Latino mother and African American father, had the most beautiful eyes, gorgeous brown complexion, and playfully curly hair. I was indeed happy to be distracted by this cute and happily chatty kid.

## 03:10 P.M.

I began heading to the tour bus, exhausted and half-asleep after all the walking and overeating the most delicious meal, and, honestly, to get away from yet another offer of tequila, which I now understand is Mexican water. But my thoughts as I returned to the bus were interrupted by that same voice that had welcomed me when I arrived at Chichen Itza; it was Habeeb and his boy, and again there was no woman in sight. Oh well, that must be the way they roll, or perhaps she is lugging a heavy pregnancy and a stroller with a set of twins with her, so she is unable to keep up with her man and a toddler. My mental monologue was quickly interrupted by his voice again as he said, "We have been looking everywhere for you. Or I should say my son has been looking everywhere for you." I laughed and asked him why his son would be looking for a stranger he had just met.

"Honestly, I think you and he met in another life.

He called you mama remember? He thinks you look like his mother."

"Oh well, that's a compliment I suppose, I can only hope she takes it as such too."

"Well, we won't ever know," he said.

"How about we ask her?"

"I wish we could but that won't be possible since she is dead."

And with those words, there was dead silence that seemed to last for 24 hours until I summoned up the courage to mumble, "I am sorry to hear that."

The horrified look on his face and the way he had hurried away earlier on now made sense to me. He had been shocked that his son, who was barely one year old when his wife died, called me, a woman he had never met, mama. That must have really shocked him, but that was just the beginning. If only I knew there were more shockers ahead. Indeed, these are no accidents or coincidences; just like our existence, everything happens by the beautiful design of our Creator.

Nasir, Habeeb's son, jumped into my arms the moment he saw me again. It was as if he was celebrating a miracle in his own way. I invited both of them to join me inside our tour bus as we waited for other passengers to arrive. He was quite inquisitive, asking every and any question including what I was writing in my notepad, how soon I was going to be done, if I knew how to fly a plane, if I could swim, and if I would like him to teach me when I said, "No." For the 15 or so minutes I had this kid on my lap, I almost completely ignored his dad. No doubt his kid has my heart in the palm of his hands already, but at that moment I was thankful for the pleasant distraction he provided. How could I not be? I didn't know whether it was appropriate to ask about Nasir's mom's death or just pretend I did not even have that awkward conversation with him at all. I was just thankful for the distracting and exciting conversation with Nasir.

The only time Habeeb joined our conversation, which both of us seemed so engrossed in, was when Nasir asked why we weren't staying at the same hotel so he could teach me how to swim, and I teach him how to read big books. I hesitated, as if I was waiting for his dad to rescue me, when Habeeb said, "Okay, c'mon buddy; it's time to go to our bus so we don't get left behind. And Aunty's bus has to go soon too." It was at that moment that the most heartbreaking resistance began. The next five minutes, which seemed like an entire day, were filled with the most sorrowful tears and cries of, "No, I want to go with Mama; please, Papa, let me go with Mama."

I am certain we looked like an estranged couple having a child custody battle. The boy's cries, Habeeb's confusion, and the sad look on my speechless face couldn't have meant any other thing to a stranger watching the whole drama. No onlooker would believe me if I tried to explain this was anything short of a child custody drama let alone the truth, which was that I had barely known this kid for five hours. He held on to my blouse and scarf in his last bid to avoid being taken away. The only thing I could do was write my hotel name, room number, and name on a piece of paper for his dad to hold on to just in case they wanted to come by to visit later on. I would certainly be honored and happy to see Nasir again, and, honestly, Habeeb too.

Habeeb looked at the paper and declared with joy that our hotels were on the same strip.

"I will be there till I leave on Saturday, please don't hesitate to stop by."

"No we won't, thank you very much, Nurah. It was certainly a miracle meeting you today." And the calm look of truth, hope and relief I saw on his face in that instant told me he meant every letter of that word—miracle.

I barely heard his words, which were drowned out by Nasir's crying.

I looked away as they moved away from the bus because, at this point, Nasir wasn't the only one crying. I had to hide my tears from Habeeb as well.

I made a silent, but desperate, heartfelt request to God to see them again soon. This couldn't be the end of our relationship, which had just begun today but had somehow grown roots as strong as the Iroko tree, the giant of the African forest.

As our bus navigated its way back to Cancun, I gazed at the ancient buildings, sandy roads filled with weeds, and street hawkers trying to entice motorists; they had my gaze but my head continued thinking about how the past six hours had gone down. I had come to see the Chichen Itza, which Bim told me was a must-see but instead I found my son, the one I never knew I had. I silently agreed with Habeeb that this was indeed a miracle. There were hundreds of people at Chichen Itza today, but somehow my path had managed to cross that of Habeeb and Nasir who live in Maryland just like me, but who I would probably never have met at home. I knew this encounter was on purpose, because there aren't coincidences in my world, there are only God-Incidences.

## 07:00 P.M.

We returned to Cancun five minutes ago. The drive into the city made me so envious—the beach, the lagoon, and the entire landscape is just like Lagos Nigeria's Ikoyi, Victoria Island and Lekki up to Epe. If the Mexicans can do that, what's stopping us? I learned that the Mexican government created five tourist towns in zones including Cancun only recently in 1970. So what's our problem? As the bus approached the Riu, Roberto thanked us for choosing to spend our vacation in Mexico and urged us to tell our friends back home that contrary to all the media reports that Mexico is unsafe we had a good time here. He said, "As you can see, this is perfectly safe, right?" as if looking to us for validation, and I nodded in agreement. He admitted that there are some problems in the northern part of the country, but these were under control. Wasn't this the same issue with Nigeria? I almost feel as if it benefits certain nations that the western media continuously exaggerate the problems in pockets of locations in countries such as Nigeria, Mexico, and the rest of the developing world. At least I think this makes them look like the only safe places to visit. Okay, enough world politics! I don't need that toxic energy to ruin this blissful vacation.

Now in Room 412 at the Riu, I am looking at the blue and green ocean with love, and listening to the happy chatter and splashes of the adults turned kids in the pool below.

I finished my prayers and promptly left the comfort of the air-conditioned room to join other beach lovers. I got on the boardwalk at the right time to welcome the sunset. I have to say this: shame on anyone who has never seen the sheer miracle of a sunset or even sunrise over the ocean. It is so beautiful to watch, your heart does a type of dance your body cannot dare to try. It is absolutely beautiful and breathtaking to see the sun return home behind the clouds as the ocean goes to sleep.

I spent some time watching the sleeping waves, the photographers, both the ones armed with all sorts of selfie sticks and the innocent bystanders whose walks on the beach were hijacked to help begging tourists capture their moments in the spotlight. Every click and flash that went off around me made me thankful I was free of the burden of cameras this time around. Don't get me wrong; there is no way I am leaving this place with only the pictures in my head. Come on, I have to have something I can touch and feel. So I have my photo shoot at the hotel tomorrow, which should cure my hunger for photos; the rest will have to stay in my heart. It is just so liberating to be able to take all the beauty in without the constant urge to document it with gadgets.

On my way to dinner, I stopped by the photo desk to confirm my appointment for tomorrow and there was an older woman lamenting about her photos. She said her husband was squinting in most of them. As I listened to her go on and on about the matter, I moved a little closer to see what the fuss was all about. My verdict? I thought the squinting was the least of the issues with the photos: I mean why did they both look so grumpy and unhappy? Why couldn't they try their best to dress a bit nicer? I mean, if you are going to go through the trouble of a professional photo shoot, you at least owe it to yourself to show up looking like you want to capture great memories. And could her bald husband have shaved his head for this trip or just the photo shoot?

"Oh, Nurah! Stop it already!"

What right do I have to make up silly judgments in my head?

All these must be signs that I am hungry or at least my brain needs some sugar. So it's time to go off to Don Roberto's for dinner now and then to my room to get dressed for the Riu African show at 09:45 p.m.

Wait a minute! Please tell me why this man, dripping wet with a clinging shirt and shorts looking like something from the set of "Maria de Los Angeles" is saying, "Hello," and winking at me. (Sigh!)

*Dem tell you say na your type I dey find?* (English translation – Did they tell you I was searching for your type?)

Dinner was largely uneventful except that, as I have been doing all through this week, I ate too much. I had better embark on a month long fasting and detox routine when I get back to reality because I must have added 20 pounds of belly fat on this trip alone. (Huge sigh!) By the way, I think this problem I am having, overeating that is, is actually not my fault. There are no clocks in the resort restaurant, so I just keep eating and eating oblivious of the time. Well, this is my story and I am sticking to it.

## 08:35 P.M.

After that heavy dinner, I knew the responsible and humane thing to do for my body was to take a walk along the hotel zone. I took a left turn out of the hotel and my eyes beheld the manmade **creation** of the hotel zone at night, with all its lights shining brightly just like Times Square but without the noise, traffic, and crowd. Walking along the strip was safe and peaceful until I saw two vicious cats, one chasing the other, and that was my cue; I knew it was time to go back to the land of human beings.

As I walked back, I noticed fellow pedestrians included not just tourists but those hotel workers who were going back to their families obviously fatigued from serving tourists like me all day for modest pay. There were women selling woven bracelets and coin purses by the sidewalk; they seemed to map out territories and gateless boundaries for each woman. Many of them had children strapped on their backs or sucking as they sold their wares. My mind traveled to Lagos, Nigeria; these women would be constantly raided by area boys (touts) or police if they were to attempt this in Victoria Island. But the flip side is that the women would be bothering and tugging at tourists if this was Lagos, unlike the ones here who sit still waiting to be approached by interested buyers.

It was only when I returned to the hotel feeling less than accomplished that I admitted the truth to myself. I hadn't taken the walk because I had overeaten and needed to walk off the calories, I had taken that walk because I was hoping to run into Habeeb and Nasir, not one or the other, but both of them; they were a good and complete package that I hadn't ever imagined prior to meeting them today, but now that they were here, they fit into my dreams seamlessly. I was about to "buy one, and get one free." Habeeb had said their hotel was close to mine, but he hadn't said which hotel was theirs. Maybe he didn't want me to know. Perhaps he has bought Nasir some ice cream and bribed him with a dip in the pool and both of them have forgotten about me. Well then, I have to get them out of my mind as well. All the scenes and acts that I had built up in my mind made me feel so silly now, I needed to come to terms with the fact that all the interaction at Chichen Itza was simply a nice day at the park; there was nothing more to it.

But why was my heart reluctant to align with my head?

## 11:00 P.M.

Wow! The African show at the Riu was spectacular! It was so amazing! I am so glad I stayed beyond the first five minutes when the acrobatic performers were doing whatever it was they were doing on the poles. I had been so angry that I almost got up to leave. The roomful of white folks were cheering and clapping happily but all I kept thinking was: *this is why these* oyinbo *people* (the Nigerian term used to describe Caucasians) *keep thinking we are all monkeys that swing and live in trees!* But honestly, after that, things picked up and the energy and skills of all the performers lit up the dark theater with every single act. I was very sad when the show ended. Like this holiday, I wanted the show to keep going on and on. At some point during the show though, I saw two

African guys pull out their smartphones to record the performances, and I felt sorry for them. If only they knew that they had switched off their hearts to rely on a device that could never capture the moments they were trying to hold on to. Maybe someday they will learn what I am learning now: that an uninterrupted connection of the eyes and the heart is all we need to capture our most powerful moments.

I know I have been bashing cameras and smartphones so you are probably thinking that I will never use them again, well, that's not even close to the truth. I think these devices have their roles; it's the obsession with them that I am trying to wean myself off to be honest. It's the urge to whip them out every time to the extent that they replace the mind that I am trying to divorce. I bet if I had my camera out trying to record every moment, I wouldn't remember how they made me feel a week from today, and that is the feeling I want to be fully present in, so that I can replay them when I get back to real life.

Anyway, back to the fabulous show: The MC really didn't need to say, "Applauso," before the entire theater gave the performers a big round of applause. In fact, the obviously drunk white lady sitting in front of me gave a standing ovation, which was actually well deserved.

I took a stroll on the beach after the show because I didn't want the night to end. I wasn't ready for the feelings of relaxation and joy to fade away just yet. The beach was quiet: two ladies walking and a couple sitting close together gazing at the stars perhaps. The waves were calm, just making enough sounds to let me know they weren't asleep. The mood was right and perfect for me to get my feet wet for the first time since I arrived in Cancun. I took off my slippers and allowed the ocean to greet my feet as I walked casually into the water. At some point, I stood still, staring at the ocean but actually seeing nothing— no colors, it just looked like I was standing in front of a quiet road, and it was tempting. I was tempted to walk on the road, but I wasn't deceived.

**The ocean's calmness at night is not a convincing reason for a sane person to test its depth.**

I turned around and walked up to room 412; Day three was over, holiday cut in half. Reality was fast approaching, and it was scary! I almost gave into the wave of fear that rushed to greet me as I opened the door to allow it inside my head. Here I was on vacation after quitting my six-figure, highflying job. What was my plan exactly? What will happen when my little savings run out? I quietly but quickly slammed the door against my fears. I will deal with those questions with a relaxed mind and rejuvenated soul when I return to Baltimore on Saturday evening. For now, I will focus on building a life that will be strong enough to make a living.

Ganiyah Tope Fajingbesi

# *Your Why*

*Would you sing a different song,*

*If you thought about the why?*

*Would you say another prayer,*

*If you didn't think about the what?*

*What exactly would you long for?*

*Hope for,*

*Wish for,*

*Cry for,*

*If you just take a moment,*

*To think about YOUR why?*

# Lights! Camera! Love!

**Thursday August 27ᵗʰ 2015**
**07:45 A.M.**

I have been awake for two hours and, apart from the 15 or so minutes that I spent saying my prayers inside my suite, I have been on the balcony greeting the ocean, praising and worshipping the one who created all this in His majesty without help from anyone and anything. It's honestly hard to deny the existence of a higher power when you witness the powerful way the sun and the ocean, two amazing forces, meet and greet. When your heart sees the sun use its light to wake up the colors of the ocean and you see the ocean return the salutation by using its gentle breeze to cool off the heat of the sun, you have to know there is a force that makes this type of magic happen; you have to agree that force is God.

There are lovers strolling, solo tourists walking, and birds working their routes along the beach and the skies. So blissful and beautiful, I wish it could last forever. I wish I could just open the doors a little bit and bring my loved ones into this life right now because I miss my sisters, nieces, and nephews so much this morning. I woke up imagining how tough it would be to get Friendly Folly out of the water, to get Professor Moro to stop exclaiming and wowing like an old philosopher and how the damsels of 2008 —Teni, Tammy and MojMoj—would have made a soap opera from this entire experience. No point wondering, I have to find out, I have to bring them here soon.

But guess what? I also miss my new family, Habeeb and Nasir. I may never see or hear from them again, but they will always have a special place in my heart. Meeting them yesterday was like watching a diver jump into the calm ocean; you know that splash it makes? That's exactly what happened yesterday. Those two made a splash in my calm heart; they woke up a part I thought was completely dead and buried. I pray I see them again, I really do!

I brought out my "Accepted Whispers" prayer book, flipped to the prayers for Thursday, and there they were, prayers about hope, children, family, wishes, and divine possibilities. Exactly what I needed! *Ameen! Mui bien. Muchas gracias, Ya Allah*.

**10:35 A.M.**
**Riu Lobby**

I just left my room for my photo shoot appearing like something out of a magazine; in fact, I should just be on the cover of *OWN*, *Ebony*, or *Essence* right about now. This shoot is going to capture my entire vacation experience in 15 shots, so I had to go the extra mile. I chose a blue dress made by the super creative and talented Mariam Gold, its color is in sync with the ocean, the texture agrees with the cool breeze, and my blue-studded hijab aligns with the ensemble. I felt like a superstar during the shoot!

I stepped into the lobby after the shoot and there they were, standing tall like perfect miracles right from heaven: Habeeb and Nasir. Nasir was trying to break free so he could run up to me; of course, I stretched out my arms and wrapped him right where he belonged. I had missed this kid so much, hard to believe I just met him a couple of hours ago. They had been there watching the photo session. Oh my goodness! I felt quite embarrassed and self-conscious now. Habeeb had seen my display of vanity in full color. Oh well! I can only hope he was smiling while watching my drama.

I knelt down so that Nasir and I could be the same height as he stayed in my arms and, more importantly, my heart. It honestly took what seemed like several minutes for me to remember that Nasir was not there alone. Habeeb greeted me warmly and it was when I looked up to respond to him that I noticed her. Oh my goodness! There she was looking stunning and beautiful as if it was her not me who just finished a photo shoot; only she didn't have to try as hard as I had to. She was in her twenties and a size-4 package. How could I even compete with this? What in the world was I thinking? Of course, a great looking guy like Habeeb with a young son would not be on the shelf for a long time. (Huge sigh!) A rush of disappointment enveloped me as I realized that all the daydreaming was just me exercising my heart as usual. But why in the world did he have to bring her here though? Why did he have to ruin the castle I was building in my head? Perhaps he had noticed my huge crush on him yesterday and he wanted to set things straight before I continued my free fall.

The depressing monologue in my head was interrupted by Habeeb's calm and rather vague introduction.

"Nurah, this is Titi."

I quickly put my face together, forced a smile, and said a silent prayer that no one heard the drama my mind has been acting for the past 60 seconds.

"It's nice to meet you, Titi."

I held myself back from adding, "And what is Titi's role in your life?"

I quickly wrapped my crazy thoughts up in a tight bag and turned to Habeeb. "It's so good to see you all this morning. I forgot to ask what hotel you are staying at."

"Oh, we are at the Dreams, just next to the Fiesta Americana."

Imagine, they are actually right next door to the Riu Palace. Instead of taking a left turn out of the hotel yesterday, I might have seen them if I had taken a right turn.

*Enough, Nurah, stop the what-ifs. The guy is here with his lady, he is taken.*

I asked them if they were hungry and wanted to join me for breakfast, and they said yes. We grabbed some food from El Romaro and sat on the beach for an impromptu picnic.

Nasir couldn't wait to get wet though; it was a struggle to get him to finish his food before he jumped into the water with Aunty Titi, as he called her. Interesting he called her Aunty but still called me Mama.

Perhaps I still stand a chance here. If the child loves me, perhaps his father may follow suit.

*Follow suit? You mean dump the size 4 'I am a model without even trying' Titi for you? Really Nurah, you need to get it together.*

Habeeb's cool voice snapped me out of my monologue one more time before I could finish building and demolishing my sandcastles any further.

"We called you a couple of times last night but it seemed you were having a late night of fun in Cancun."

"Oh! I am sorry, I didn't know you called; I went to watch the fantastic African show at the hotel theatre and later took a short walk on the beach."

"Oh, no need to apologize; we are the ones who

should be sorry for barging in on you and literally stalking you. We are probably ruining your getaway; but Nasir cried himself to sleep yesterday and he began asking for you at 5 a.m. today."

"Then the feeling is mutual because he made quite an impression on me yesterday and I woke up thinking about him too. I bet this must be a challenge for you, though, him getting attached to strange women."

"You know, that's the strangest thing. He is honestly very shy around people he doesn't know. So him and you, I mean all that stuff yesterday completely shocked me."

I laughed and told him how horrified he looked yesterday, which made him laugh too. I stole a quick glance at him, our gaze met briefly, his eyes were just the most amazing, and electric eyes I had ever seen. Oh! I wish he were single.

That moment, which I wanted to last forever, was interrupted by his phone.

"Sorry, I have to get this."

I appreciated the break time to get myself together, saved by the bell indeed! His conversation was short; he gave the person at the other end a description of where we were. "That was my brother; he is coming to meet us so we can go to the water park with the kids."

While Titi and Nasir built castles with the beach sand, Habeeb and I talked about everything and anything. Nasir didn't seem to need me when he had Titi, and that made me slightly jealous. Although he did run to his dad and me once in a while as if to check that I was still there and not going anywhere.

Habeeb is 34 years old, arghh! Four years younger than I am. His late wife died shortly after Nasir was born, making him a widower at 30 years old. He was devastated; he quit his job at a law firm to focus on his son and grow his passion, travels and tourism in developing countries, into a travel agency business. He and his family were in Cancun for a family wedding holiday on Saturday night.

"Oh, here you are!"

His brother was here, and that broke my heart because I wanted the conversation to continue forever. So what if he is not single and available? Titi didn't seem to mind him spending these couple of minutes with me anyway. She was happy to be bonding with her future stepson anyway.

"Nurah, meet Alli, my younger brother, Titi's husband."

Oh, my goodness! Can you see my heart and head exploding with relief and joy? Did this dude just say Titi wasn't his wife? Did you hear my chances just go back up? Did you see me just relocate from the dumpster to the mansion? I almost got on my head to do some cartwheels. I almost laughed aloud with great relief, but I kept my composure, Alhamdulillah.

Maybe, just maybe he had brought Titi along to distract Nasir so he and I could get a chance to talk? Hmmmmmm…

"Alright, buddy, enough. Let's go to the waterpark, your cousins are waiting." Habeeb rallied Nasir, who didn't resist too much this time around, perhaps because he knew that he would see me again. He hugged me and said, "See you later, Mama."

"See you later, sweetie," I replied before planting a kiss on his forehead.

"Do you have plans for tonight?" I asked Habeeb, not sure where the boldness came from.

"Nothing that can't be cancelled," he said.

"How about dinner around 7 p.m.?"

"Perfect. I can meet you in your lobby and we can decide where to go."

"Sounds good. Alli and Titi can come as well."

"Oh no! Two is company, four is a crowd." That was Titi with a mischievous smile on her face.

Day 4 in Cancun could not have begun on a brighter note!

I was still in my blue dress when I made my way to the entertainment area to find the venue for the Spanish class. I knew people were staring at me because I was all dressed up when almost everyone else was practically naked. I was watching my steps to be sure I didn't fall down and become the laughing stock of the hotel, when a lady clad in a bikini rushed up to me asking if she could take a picture with me. I said yes and silently hoped she didn't see me as some African princess or other such spectacle lest I end up on some Argentinian blog tomorrow morning. Anyway, an innocent passerby took two shots with the lady's phone and I made my way to the entertainment center in peace.

Juan scheduled me for a noon Spanish class after asking me what my goals were. He, like so many other people here and back home, asked me if I was British, and I said no for the millionth time in my 38-year life. I asked him where he was from, and he said that he moved to Cancun from Fredericksburg, Virginia.

"Really? I live in Baltimore, Maryland."

"Oh, I know where that is, I used to go there all the time."

"So why did you move to Cancun?"

He used his eyes to scan the pool, beach, and people enjoying life and said the obvious, "I moved for this life."

And that truly made sense. Life in Virginia or anywhere in the USA is certainly different from life in Cancun. I could certainly not blame him.

I continued repeating his words, "*I moved for this life,*" as I walked to the concierge to make dinner reservations. What move am I willing to make for the life I am meant to live?

My good friend at the concierge desk looked at me with something that ranged between admiration and flirtation.

"Oh! There comes my friend from Nigeria."

"Ekaabo" welcomed me with the Yoruba greeting I had taught him on Tuesday.

"How do I say *beautiful* in your language?"

I hesitated because I knew he wanted to use it for me. But when he wouldn't let me off the hook and book me for the dinner I came to reserve, I taught him and he giddily declared, "O rewa," meaning *I am beautiful.*

I hurriedly replied, "Muchas gracias," and changed the topic to the African show at the hotel last night. I am no Stella trying to get her groove back in Cancun please.

I made my way back to 412, not just to change my dress so that the whole hotel could stop thinking I am the Queen of Africa, but I also needed to select the best outfit to wear for my dinner "date" with Bibi tonight.

Oh, yes! I already have a nickname for the guy I just met yesterday. Lord help me!

I had a massage and facial at the Bamboo spa, right across from the Riu. Not only did it cost 50% less than the Riu, but I can almost say for certain that Gloria (facial) and Isabella (massage) are the best game in town. The experience was very relaxing and exactly what I needed after taking a ten-minute bashing from the Cancun sun.

However, after the internet connection problems, which made it impossible for the spa to charge my visa card, and my inability to make a simple telephone connection, I can safely declare that Mexico may be light years ahead of Nigeria when it comes to tourism, but in terms of telecoms, we are neck and neck.

So why am I sitting here missing my family? Why does it feel like I haven't spoken to my sisters in years? I really like this as an "off grid" vacation, but give me two days and I begin craving my regular chats with my siblings, especially my sisters. I tried calling them from the hotel, I honestly didn't mind the two-dollar per minute cost, but I couldn't get through.

If only I knew that missing my sisters and being unable to reach them on the phone was just the beginning of my troubles in Cancun on day 4, perhaps I would have put on my big girl pants earlier on.

*No is the only sure answer you will get if you don't ask. Be Bold.*

## 02:00 P.M.

If I can't experience the thrill of selling Cancun to my sisters on the phone, I might as well dream about meeting up with Bibi tonight, right? And that's what my mind was preparing to embark upon when I saw a note at the front desk saying I had a message from Senor Habeeb.

"Hola senorita."

"Hola."

"Senor Habeeb called you, he can't meet again tonight, he said maybe tomorrow. But he will call you later to talk to you."

Are you seriously kidding me right now? I felt like a bloated balloon that had just been attacked by a tiny needle. Someone needs to help me rescue day 4 because the bricks are certainly falling hard and fast. Why did he cancel? Perhaps he sensed my desperation when I asked what he was doing tonight. I just keep messing everything up with this forwardness, don't I? I should know that men, regardless of race or status, like to be the hunters, and not the hunted. Oh! I wish I would think first before speaking sometimes. But I thought he fancied me as well, or did I read him wrong? Was he just nice because his son thinks I am his dead mother reincarnated? Or maybe he realized that he is younger than I am, but I didn't say anything when he said his age.

"Of course, you didn't need to say anything, Nurah! Your face is as easy to read as a kindergarten storybook."

So he saw my relief when he introduced Alli as Titi's husband, he sensed my eagerness to see him again and perhaps saw my bonding with his son as a ploy to trap him after barely 24 hours of meeting him. How did a solo vacation become so complicated? I mean, I am a veteran solo vacationer; these trips are usually about me and me alone. How did I get to this point?

I am just going to forget him; I will simply reset my clock to the blissful moments before he and his adorable son barged into my life. After all, he doesn't fit the package anyway. Yes, he is tall and fine, but he has a child already and, please, I am not going to compete with the memories of a dead high school sweetheart. No one wins a wrestling match against a ghost, much less the shadow of a ghost.

And with that win of my head over my aching heart, I switched on the television, there had to be something to send me to a sound sleep on there. And that, dear diary, turned out to be a bad idea! The TV has eight channels—four in Spanish and the other four in English. So why would the four English channels be a bad idea? Well, wait until you read what they are: BBC, CNN, Fox, and CNN Headline News. Five minutes flipping through and I knew why watching TV in Cancun is not advisable. In just five minutes, or less in fact, I had caught up on the world's tales of woe—a gunman who killed two journalists on live TV in my neighboring state of Virginia, the global financial doom driven by the Chinese, the migrant crisis in Europe affecting Syrians and other middle easterners trying to flee the region's turmoil, and so many other horrible realities of our world. By the time the BBC decided to read the good news about Usain Bolt's double win at Beijing I was already mentally down and out. It was so bad that I could not even muster a fraction of my typical excitement about my favorite athlete's victory.

The sad thing about watching the news is not even how horrible the sad tales make you feel, but for me, on this fantasy beach vacation, news is the reality check I could do without. I realized that the news was making me have nightmares while awake in the middle of the day; I began thinking about how broke I may become if I don't decide what to do next, how many voicemails and emails will be waiting for me when I get home, how much money our charity still has to raise for our back-to-school program for low income kids in Nigeria. The Riu Palace must have made the TV lineup crappy on purpose so everyone will get out of their rooms and spend time on the beach, but I couldn't take the beach pill right now. I don't need to see lovers talking, strolling and having fun when my heart is aching. I will just take the pill that works to calm me down every single time—sleep!

I woke up around 06:00 p.m., washed my face, and went downstairs to check out my photos. Cristina Moreno, the talented photographer who shot the photos, had left for the day, but I met Priscila Aguire, yet another Hispanic-American who had moved back to Mexico from the USA. If all you went by was the cable news and all you listened to was Donald Trump's hateful comments about immigrants, you would never believe that there are Mexicans leaving the USA for Mexico; you would think all Mexicans were lining up at the U.S. border posts trying to enter illegally. I had already spoken with two Mexicans who moved back home within four days of being at the Riu alone. Imagine how many I would find if I expanded my scope beyond the hotel. Anyway, let's leave the politics of immigration alone.

I started browsing through the photos from my shoot and the first problem I identified was not with the light or picture quality but how much weight I need to lose. Oh my goodness! I look so puffy. This is certainly due to all the food I have been eating even prior to Cancun—my sisters were with me for two weeks and all they did was cook and I just ate the entire time. I need a detox and a strict exercise plan as soon as I get home!

Selecting the photos to buy was tough, I was on a budget so I could only afford 15, but every one of those 63 photos was calling my name. Priscilla felt sorry for me as I flipped back and forth, eliminating some photos with pain on my face as if I was a toddler struggling to hold on to her new toy. This right here is the reason why I avoid malls and markets. I just hate making choices. It took me over an hour, but I eventually chose the 15 photos that I looked best in and went to have dinner alone. No more Bibi date remember?

And dinner at Don Roberto was exactly what the doctor recommended. Juan from the entertainment team, who was the first person to meet and greet me at the door, promised me a two-hour Spanish class tomorrow and told me to make sure I didn't miss the Michael Jackson show at the theater later tonight.

Two pills that work—sleep and food had managed to restore my falling mind. Thank you, Lord, for free gifts that are simply priceless.

## 10:30 P.M.

And the Michael Jackson show? Let's just say the cable news networks deceived us! They said the King of Pop—Michael Jackson—died. Big lie! Michael Jackson didn't die; he just got tired of the USA and moved to Cancun, Mexico!

Okay, on a serious note now, Levi Garcia, the Michael Jackson impersonator at the Riu tonight? He was phenomenal, fantastic, electric, and entertaining. I was so impressed. Even the little girl sitting next to me, who could not have seen MJ when he was alive, was in the zone as well. I was dancing on my seat and having such a good time until one of the Thriller characters appeared behind and tapped me, scaring me silly. I have heard about the good MJ impersonators in Vegas, but this Garcia guy must be the deal. The hair, voice, fit of the costumes, dance, and everything else was on point. But the weirdest part is the guy truly feels he is Michael Jackson. I could tell just by the way he addressed the audience during the intermissions. He seems to have dumped Levi Garcia's life to assume Michael Jackson's own. I am not sure if that made me feel sorry or happy for him. But there was no doubt in my mind that he put up an awesome performance.

As I took my nightly stroll on the beach, I thought about Michael Jackson, one of my favorite entertainers of all time whose death I still struggle with today. It must have been quite tough to carry all that he did in one body, one heart. To have it all yet have nothing at all is something even ordinary non-celebrities like me struggle with in my own little way.

Is that not why I am in Cancun right now, so I can be disconnected from it all?

I thought about what I will leave in the world for people to "impersonate" when I am gone.

Will I ever feel complete and content with this life God has gifted me?

Will I ever be brave enough to live the life God created me to live in full?

I left the beach and went to bed scared, really scared.

Ganiyah Tope Fajingbesi

# Seduction

*You don't know what seduction is until you have seen the*
*ocean,*
*Seduction is not a naked woman trying to lure her prey,*
*Seduction is the ocean at dawn when it wakes the palm trees*
*With its breeze gently yet suggestively swaying ashore.*

*Seduction is the ocean in the still of the night*
*When it lures the walker with its sweet, beautiful lips*
*With warm kisses on her feet urging her to let go.*

*Seduction is the warm embrace in the heart*
*Tight yet not strong enough to choke,*
*It's the nod of acceptance of the palm trees*
*As though calling and urging in voices so low*
*Yet the non-swimmer can hear louder than the mermaid.*
*Seduction is the art of temptation only the ocean has mastered.*

# *Now That We Found Love*

**Friday August 28th 2015**
**07:00 A.M.**

My sizzling love affair watching the sunrise from the balcony was cut short by the sound of the phone ringing in my suite. I leapt off the floor with joy to grab the phone before it cut off. I was certain the caller was bringing me joy this morning, and I was right!

"Buenos dias, Senorita."

"Good Morning."

"I have Bola on the line for you, should I transfer?"

"Si, gracias, Senor," I replied in my little Spanish with Nigerian accent.

"De nada."

And that is how the morning of day 5 started, on a high note with my sisters ushering in sunshine. We chatted, laughed, and bonded for over an hour, or shall I say I went on and on about how awesome Cancun is but how their absence made it incomplete? I was completely famished by the time I got off the phone so I went to Don Roberto restaurant where Juan, who has practically become my personal waiter this week, greeted me with his signature warm smile that lit up my mind. Not only did he seat me in the quietest corner of the room with breathtaking views of the ocean, he also got my drinks—fruit juice and tea—without me telling him. He already knew what I wanted, awesome guy! Why can't breakfast in Baltimore or Lagos be like this all the time? Okay, maybe all the time is asking for too much, but it would be nice to do this every now and then you know? The only downside to breakfast was overeating of course! My attempt to eat just a little didn't quite work out, as usual. (Sigh!)

By the time I got to my room, Angela, the lovely lady who cleans my room, was there so I met her for the first time this week. She had barely left the room when my attempt to go take a shower, wash my hair and head over to Spanish class was foiled by the phone. I assumed it must be my sisters again.

"Hello! I thought both of you were going shopping."

"Hi Nurah. It's Habeeb."

"Oh! Sorry, I thought it was my sisters calling

back." I rushed out the words because my heart literarily skipped several beats.

And that, ladies and gentlemen, is how day 5 in Cancun became full of the fireworks that made the Olympics opening ceremony seem like child's play.

"Sorry to barge in like this so early, but do you have a moment?"

"Sure," I answered almost with a stammer.

"Can you come down to the lobby in about ten minutes?"

"Sure, but let's make it 15 - 20 minutes. You don't want to see me in this state," I said as I laughed nervously.

"Alright, see you soon. Insha Allah!"

I jumped into the shower with excitement and changed my clothes an endless number of times. I didn't want to be overdressed, or appear too simple. I eventually settled for a simple yet beautiful turquoise dress to match the mood of the calm Cancun Ocean.

Bibi was already downstairs by the time I stepped out of the elevator. *Oh, my goodness, this guy looks even finer than he did the first two times I saw him.* As soon as I saw him though, I quickly brought out the invisible wall of coldness, that wall I erect when people are getting close enough to choke life out of me. Only this time, I was not choked by this beautiful gift of God in front of me. Remember all that talk about him being younger, with a child, and me not wanting to compete with a dead wife? It was all flying into the bottom of the ocean with every step I took towards him.

So what if he is younger? He seems mature and can certainly teach me a lot. And in which country's law is it an offense to have a child, especially one that fell in love with me at first sight? And all that thought of him being married before, for goodness sake, Nurah; you are not even the one to talk. You were once married too and he also has to contend with the ghost of that turbulent period of your life. I had scripted an entire soap opera by the time I sat on the chair next to the coffee table at the lobby almost across from him.

"I am so sorry I couldn't make it last night. The airline lost the suitcase containing the groomsmen's clothes for the wedding ceremony."

"Oh, my goodness," I interrupted with laughter that expressed relief more than humor. Thank God he hadn't called off our date (or shall I call it something else?) because he didn't like me or because he felt I was too desperate. I quickly pressed pause on my daydreams to listen to the groomsmen's suit drama. He told me how they had to drive around town with the event planner until late at night looking for something for the groomsmen to wear, but they eventually got a call from the airline informing them that the missing suitcase had been located and would be delivered to the hotel today.

We must have sat there for close to two hours. As

with many places in this resort, there was no clock in sight so it was difficult to know how fast time was flying by. The conversation, however, started on a very sober note. I told Bibi about my five-minute encounter with reality yesterday when I switched on the TV to watch the news; he told me there was more bad news; about 200 people, also migrants from Syria and Africa, died when their boat sank in the Mediterranean. We spoke at length about how blessed we are to be free from the unimaginable level of hardship our fellow human beings are facing across the globe. My heart sank as I thought about "the troubles" I thought I had; the troubles I was running away from in Maryland, which made me take annual escapes to the beach. We talked about how these were actually not troubles at all; instead they were simply perks of the charmed life I was living, the privileged life we were living.

Bibi reminded me that, even if the people displaced by the Boko Haram crisis in Northern Nigeria or the war in Syria had plane tickets to the beach, which was highly unlikely, they wouldn't be able to leave their troubles behind, as all that sorrow seemed to follow them everywhere they went - quite sad. Honestly, I was falling in love with this man sitting across from me, who wasn't whining, lamenting, forcing, reprimanding, or condescending in any way, but was helping me see how blessed and extremely fortunate we were to be gifted with this life we had.

We began talking about how we could help these

people, our own brothers and sisters, and their kids who rode on the backs of trucks, in bad boats and trekked for days at midnight while we slept or dipped our feet into the cool embrace of the ocean. We had a duty to help our siblings who embarked on the journey of uncertainty, unsure of the reception, if any, that their host cities would give them; unsure whether they would even make it to their destinations alive. It is not enough to feel pity for them, to chastise their oppressors at home and the predators who exploit them and mastermind their unsafe passage at sea. What we need to do is reach out in a small way, whichever that was, to send some of the love we have their way. It was during this soul-inspiring encounter with Bibi that a big light bulb switched on in my mind —I decided to publish and sell this diary.

"You know, I have an idea of how we can help."

"Nice, tell me about it," he said, as his eyes lit up with the type of hope that made my heart leap.

"I have been keeping a diary since I started this trip. What if I turn it into a book, sell it, and donate part of the proceeds to help the people displaced by the Boko Haram crisis in Nigeria, the Syrian refugees and, of course, my kids at United for Kids Foundation?" I said, as I brought out my diary from my purse.

I noticed the hope in his eyes had now turned into curiosity, but I continued anyway. "The two things I love to do, especially when I am stressed out, are traveling, or more like escaping and writing, which is another vehicle that takes me to a safe space. Imagine if I could use these tools that work like magic for me to rally people, another gift God has given me, to help a million people escape their troubles somehow."

I wanted to go on and on about how I could donate proceeds to displaced adults in Northern Nigeria, launch cooperatives so they could earn money to provide for their families and rebuild their towns, how I could donate some proceeds to help reliable aid agencies provide relief to Syrian migrants and a lot more. My brain was working like a machine now. I was in my "save the world" mode, but I couldn't continue because Bibi now had the most mischievous grin on his face. I hardly found what I was saying funny, so why was he grinning like a child?

"What? Why are you looking at me like that? You don't think it's a good idea?"

"No. I think it's an excellent idea. In fact, something tells me you are a good writer, but let's start from the part of you keeping a diary, meaning you have been writing about everything that has happened since you got here on Monday?"

"Well, only notable things," I replied.

"Hmmm, did you consider meeting me to be a notable thing?" he asked as he turned his head sideways with that mischievous grin on his face again.

"Actually no, I didn't consider meeting you a notable thing." I paused to look at the expression on his face. He was no longer grinning; he had a plain, almost sad look of a man rejected on his face.

"I consider meeting you a miracle. So, yes, you and Nasir are featured in my diary, if that's what you are asking."

"Oh wow!" His look had changed to that of a toddler in a toy store. He was beaming with excitement now.

"Can I read what you wrote about me?"

"Of course not!" I said, feeling a little bit embarrassed. I was not ready for him to know I liked him or that I was sad when he canceled yesterday or that I already had a nickname for him! There was way too much in this diary he just couldn't find out about yet.

"But the whole world is going to read it!"

"Well yes! But at that time, I will be ready to share. They are mostly good things though, I promise."

"I don't believe you. Tell me one thing you wrote."

"Okay, just one thing!"

"Yes one thing, but, Nurah, it has to be a big thing!"

"What is big, now you are asking with conditions?"

"I mean don't tell me, 'Habeeb wore a blue shirt.' I'd rather hear something I don't already know."

"Okay, here you go! This is as big as it gets. That your son called me mama the first time he saw me and that made my heart full of joy."

He seemed to take forever to respond or show any emotion. I was getting worried that I had touched a raw spot when he said, "You think meeting me was a miracle, Nurah? Honestly, being at the bus park, seeing you, watching the whole world stand still make miracles seem like a simple word. And seeing the instant connection between you and Nasir was … it was…"

His phone rang at that moment, and I saw relief all over his face, as if, just as my phone had saved me yesterday, the same rescue had just happened to him, only this time I was pained. I wanted him to continue; that heaviness in his voice and the tender look I had spotted on his face could only mean one thing.

I could see the signs really clearly. We were both falling in love in Cancun.

He finished his phone call with the words, "I am on my way."

And my heart broke; he had to go?

We had only just begun. I felt a strong wave of sadness wash over me.

"I can't believe I have been here for two hours. The groomsmen's suits have been delivered and everyone is looking for me. I have to go and try mine on. You know this wedding business." He laughed.

"Sure." I managed not to sound bothered by the interruption.

"But if it's not too much to ask and you don't have other plans, would you like to come with my cousins, Alli, and me for dinner tonight?"

I wanted to pretend that I wasn't excited by saying I had plans, but my head clicked with my heart and I said the right thing.

"Sure. I can't think of a better way to wrap up my Cancun vacation."

"I will walk over here at 06:30 p.m. then."

"Sounds good. See you, insha Allah."

My mind leapt for joy as I walked towards the elevators. I knew he was watching me, so I did not do my happy dance until I was safely behind the closed doors inside the elevator.

As I rode up, I thought about the pink dress Mama Moses made for me the last time I was in Nigeria. It had seemed out of place when I placed it in my Cancun luggage, but now I knew it was not in my suitcase by accident.

There would be fireworks in Cancun tonight; I could feel it already.

I was ready for dinner at 06:15 p.m., but I waited in my suite until I got a call from the lobby that Bibi was downstairs.

I stepped out of the elevators looking like a million dollars.

"As-Salam Alaekum. Err, you look really beautiful, amazing, Masha Allah," he said as soon as I met him at the lobby.

"So do you, Senor. Salam to you as well."

"Shall we?"

"Sure. Where are the others?"

"They are at the restaurant, it's the Krystal."

"Oh nice! It's the place with the purple blinds? I have been curious about it, I am happy I get a chance to eat there before I leave."

Alli, Titi, and two other men were already at the Krystal when we arrived. Bibi introduced them as his cousins; they were all here for the same wedding.

"We have heard nothing else but Nurah this and that since Wednesday," gushed one of the guys named Yusuf.

"Really?" I shyly replied.

"We had to come and see for ourselves that you were real."

"Well, here I am, live and direct. I hope I don't disappoint you." I laughed.

I am certain they had planned this before we got there, because Bibi and I seemed to have room to speak privately, we had our own corner almost.

Our waiters were excellent—Rigo, a very warm gentleman with the most inviting and heartwarming smile, and Carlos, almost shy and a gentle man. They certainly added to the love in the room for sure.

We started with the most delicious tapas and salad I have ever tasted in my life. We enjoyed light conversation as we went through the appetizers, but just as the entree was about to be served, the conversation became more serious.

"You know my parents are scared that I will never re-marry."

I took my attention away from my plate to listen to him.

"And I don't blame them really. Nasir's mother's death shook me pretty hard; it was a difficult period for me indeed, a big test of my faith."

"I can imagine how hard that must have been."

"Honestly, I used to break down in tears every time I held my son. I didn't sign up for raising him without his mom. And she was such a lovely soul. You know…"

"Death is so final, it is so difficult. It's almost as though you are being cheated."

"For the first two years, I was like a zombie. Each time I thought I was recovering, something little would send me back over the hill again. I was a mess."

Then I began to pray about it at the beginning of this year; I began to trust Allah more and it helped me believe that I will be okay, that He will give me a second chance to love again."

"Indeed He is able to do that and more," I said in a very reassuring voice with belief.

"These guys and Titi," he continued after glancing in their direction briefly, "they tried to set me up with all sorts of women. They were nice, at least many were, but there was no spark. I didn't feel anything. They made so much fuss and fun about it."

"I feel you on the spark thing. Marriage is hard enough with someone you love; to be in it with someone you really have no feelings for is a nightmare."

"Exactly."

"I used to think it was a sin to fall in love, but I attended Love Notes by Sheikh Birjas last weekend and learned a lot from it. It's what you do with love that determines if it's a sin, not falling in love itself. Amazing class!"

His eyes lit up as he replied, "I took it earlier this year, and you would have thought I had no experience with marriage the way I was taking notes. It is a class everyone should take before and after marriage."

"I agree 150%."

Then his voice dropped a little bit, as if he got a bit nervous. He looked at me and then looked at his entree, which had now been served, but which neither of us had touched.

"Nurah, I have learned so much since I met you two days ago." He laughed dryly before continuing.

"The amount of prayers and research I have done these past two days, you would think I was trying to get into a Ph.D. program."

"Research and prayers about what?" I pretended as if I had no idea.

"About you, Nurah, about us, you and me." He looked at me as if trying to check if it was okay with me.

"That's not fair! I haven't had the chance to do any research about you."

"Tough luck!" His laughter had relief written all over it.

"So what did you find? I am curious."

"Well, I know you used to be in a marriage that wasn't particularly happy…"

"You don't say!" I laughed and rolled my eyes.

"You lost a pregnancy at a very advanced stage."

"Actually, make that four losses."

"Oh! Wow, I am sorry."

"What else?"

"You love kids, and that was pretty evident watching you with Nasir on day 1."

"Yeah, I love, love, love children. No wonder it's an area in which Allah tested me the most."

"And you lost your dad, your biggest cheerleader in 2014."

"Wow! You do not play around at all; you should join the FBI when you get home. But hey! Watch out for me. When I get back on the grid, I will send my sniffer dogs to dig out all there is to know about you. This is my lane!"

He cleared his throat and began in such a serious tone; I almost became scared of what would come out of his mouth.

"I hope you do, Nurah. I hope you do because I don't want to fool around. I don't date. This right here, for me, is serious. I am not looking for now, what I want—which I pray is what you want too when you pray, think and do your research about me —is forever."

And just like that, the world stood still. I wanted to say something but the words just wouldn't come out. I expected fireworks at dinner, but certainly not the magnitude of an Olympic opening ceremony. As if he sensed my handicap, he went on...

"I am not asking you to say anything right now; I don't imagine you came to Cancun to hear these words. But I had to let you know before you go home tomorrow. I hope you give it some thought."

Then I found my voice…

"Is this because your son called me mama, Habeeb? If that's it, I can help with Nasir but we don't have to complicate things."

"Nurah, no. This has absolutely nothing to do with my son."

I could almost see the hurt on his face.

"I know, it's just scary, I am just scared."

"Scared of what?"

"What if you get back home and change your mind? What if this is just some ocean breeze hangover?" I was nervous but I still managed to laugh at my choice of words.

"Isn't life full of what ifs, Nurah? But, no, this is not some ocean breeze hangover. I already had a strong feeling we would be having this discussion at some point the first day I met you, when I didn't even know all the amazing things I know now."

"I am older than you. You know that, right? I mean four years older."

"Yes, I know, but how is that a problem?"

"No, it's not a problem. I just wanted to be sure you knew that."

"I also know that you are a very busy woman, but

I am not worried about it. I will support you with everything I have got, but I also have a feeling you will put us and our love first."

"Wow! You are charming me, aren't you?

"I haven't even begun, Nurah, just wait until you are my wife and I become your biggest supporter and enabler."

"Insha Allah."

He nodded. "Insha Allah."

I had arrived in Cancun a miserable, lonely, and overworked spinster, and, in just five days, I was sitting across from the finest man Allah created, talking about a beautiful future with an adorable son as part of the package. Was this really happening or was I dreaming?

**09:00 P.M.**
**Riu Palace Las Americas**
**Poolside**

I went straight to the hotel poolside when I got back from dinner. It wasn't just the pirate ship that lit up the dark ocean that attracted me to the pool; it was also the fantasy that had just become my reality. I have always asked God to let me know my husband as soon as I meet him and vice versa. I always told Him never to make us wait, doubt, and waste time. Apparently, He was listening because all those prayers have been answered in a big way in Cancun this week.

"Pretty fascinating isn't it?"

I turned around to find a very gentle looking, beautiful lady standing behind me. She looked familiar; I remembered seeing her with the twin toddlers at the resort earlier and even at dinner with one of the twins at dinner at the Krystal.

"Yes, it's beautiful," I replied.

We talked like old friends as we enjoyed the cool breeze from the ocean. She was in her fifties, originally from India but now a Canadian from Vancouver. She told me about Isla Majeres, how beautiful it is. Her daughter, Roms, got married in Puerta Vallerta last year to a Muslim who was originally from Fiji. I asked her how she felt about that considering she is a Sikh, and that took us into a deeper conversation about marriage in her generation compared to ours. She got married at age 20 to a man her parents chose for her. Her sister, the grandmother of the beautiful twin girls, also got married to her husband's brother. She was warm, wise, and friendly. My conversation with her was exactly how I wanted to end a beautiful night. My last night in Cancun.

# Have You Ever?

*Have you ever dared to pause,*

*To hear the sound most divine?*

*Have you ever stayed still,*

*To listen to the orchestra without a band?*

*Have you ever taken a moment,*

*To feel the miracle within your soul?*

*If you have never heard yourself breathe,*

*You have never heard the soundtrack of life.*

# We've Only Just Begun

**Saturday August 29th 2015**
**05:00 A.M.**

W ow, last day in Cancun! Six days of fun, love, life and goodness. How blessed am I? Regardless of what reality holds from here on out, I know I have enough love in my own wings, thank God, to stay on top of things.

I walked over to the Dreams Hotel to observe morning prayers with Bibi and his crew.

Have you ever prayed with the ocean breeze providing the most soothing soundtrack? If you haven't, you are missing something. What a powerful connection it brings. Thank me after you try it, okay?

Bibi led the prayers, and, oh, my goodness, the sound of his voice as he recited the Quran. It was not as I had daydreamed about all these years, it was much better. Oh wow! I almost cried when we were done.

I couldn't stay with the crew for much longer; I gave Nasir a warm hug and told him I would be waiting for him at the airport when he returned on Monday.

I walked over to the beach behind the Riu to say goodbye to the ocean, which was louder this morning yet as inviting as ever. I dropped my feet in it and stood still for more than 30 minutes allowing the waves to hug my feet and the cool breeze, which in my Yoruba language will be called "Ate gun Alaafia" meaning breeze of peace, caress my face.

I changed my mind about saying goodbye to the ocean. Saying goodbye would be lying. How could I bid farewell to something that ferried so much love to me every single day? Instead I said, "See you soon."

I know I will be back here soon, insha Allah; I just have to come back.

## 10:30 A.M.
## At The Hotel Checkout Desk

"Buenos dias, Senorita."

"Buenos dias," I replied.

"I hope you enjoyed your stay in Cancun."

"It was amazing. Mucho gracias. Mucho gracias."

"I am happy to hear that."

As I turned around to leave the hotel, the concierge called out to me. "You have a package, Senorita."

*Oh! Nice,* I thought. I assumed it was the hotel's parting gift to me as I opened the rectangular, pink box.

But it wasn't. It was Bibi who had dropped off a surprise "see you later" gift for me.

And what I found in it brought tears, tears of joy, to my eyes: a beautiful gold bracelet with the inscription *Love and Light.*

Not only are those the meanings of both our names, I cannot think of other words that describe what this week meant to me other than love and light.

I stepped into my taxi with a silent prayer of gratitude to God on my lips for making my dreams come true.

We were less than two miles to the airport when my USA Transfers driver, Mr. Irineo Diaz, finally cracked the codes no other Mexican had been able to crack for the past six days. He told me the Spanish name for the telenovela I used to be obsessed with in Nigeria back in the '90s: "The Rich also Cry." It's Los Ricos Tambien Lloran; imagine, it was shot in Mexico in the '70s but we didn't watch it in Nigeria until the '90s. He also told me that "Maria de Los Angeles"— another telenovela we grew up binging on in Nigeria

—was based on Pedro Infante's black and white movie from the '40s.

He declared, as he looked at me, chuckling, through the rear view mirror, "You are a special lady because in all my life no one ever asked me this question." I thanked him for cracking the code and for wrapping up my vacation with the most enjoyable ride.

I smiled as I glanced at the bracelet already on my wrist by the time Senor Diaz dropped me off at the airport. This gesture would have freaked me out and brought out my walls this time last week, but now, as I rubbed it with joy, it actually made my heart leap again.

And that verse of the Quran that means: *"Should He not know – He that created? And He is the One that understands the finest mysteries (and) is well-acquainted (with them),"* - Quran 67:13, now made a whole load of sense to me again. Indeed, He knew all along who I needed, where and when to bring him to me.

Muchas gracias, Mexico. I promise to be back, insha Allah. But I won't come alone; I will be back with my best friends and my family. I need to help them find Love in Cancun as well.

# I Found Love

Love for God, In spite of His Invisibility.

Love for my life, In spite of my flaws.

Love for the world, In spite of its turbulence.

Love for my purpose, In spite of its challenges.

Love for my inner circle, In spite of their imperfections.

Love for the ocean, In spite of my inabilities.

Indeed, I found love in Cancun.


On its beautiful beaches,

In its gentle breeze,

And especially its amazing souls,

In Rigo when he declared,

"You make my day very happy"

And Carlos when he kept his promise to make coconut fritters
on Friday,

In Juan when he greeted me with tea and mixed fruit juice every
morning,

And in all the men and women who smiled, spoke, and
nodded,

Through them all, I found love in Cancun

# Rain On The Beach

*Have you ever watched the sky sing with the ocean?*

*Ever seen how they rave so loudly yet no one but them really feels the melody?*

*Ever watched them feed each other without a care in the world,*

*While glorifying the one who match made them?*

*The sky praising the heavens with loud roars,*

*And the ocean prostrating and bowing in adoration in its rich turquoise splendor.*

*Then which of the favors of your Lord will you deny?*

# In My Mind

I quit my job; my dad died; life was getting too complicated.

I had to throw all the pieces on the ground and rearrange my entire life. So off I went to Cancun, no phones, friends, family, computer, or camera. It was the fourth time I had taken a solo vacation since I got divorced from a marriage that lasted less than three years. I have come to find these vacations liberating and insightful, so I always take a couple of pens and notebooks to keep a journal of my thoughts.

But lying on the beach on the first day at the Riu Palace Las Americas (August 24, 2015), I decided to add my daydreams to my reality at the time; I thought about how nice it would be if I could spice up this bliss with some fantasy and imagination, to author my own destiny during these six days. The result of that process is what you have just read in this fusion of fiction, non-fiction and inspiration. It's *Love in Cancun*.

I pray that *Love in Cancun* inspires you to connect with your soul. And I hope it inspires you to speak greatness, love and success into your existence because, as I found out after writing this book, your biggest dreams can and will come true if you believe.

*Ganiyah Tope Fajingbesi*

# *Your Story*

Thank you so much for reading my story, it's now time to write yours. I hope this page inspires you to breathe life into your biggest dreams that will come true!

*"If there's a book that you want to read, but it hasn't been written yet, then you must write it."*

## —— Toni Morrison

30495586R00078